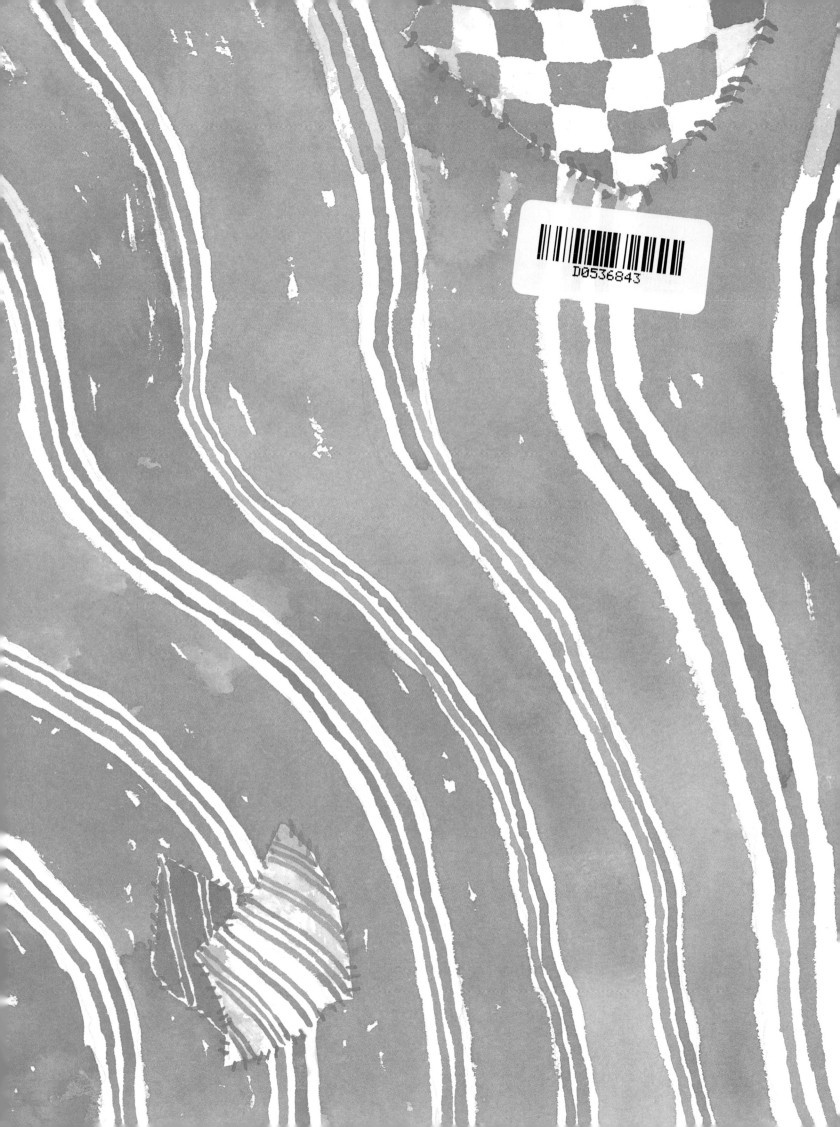

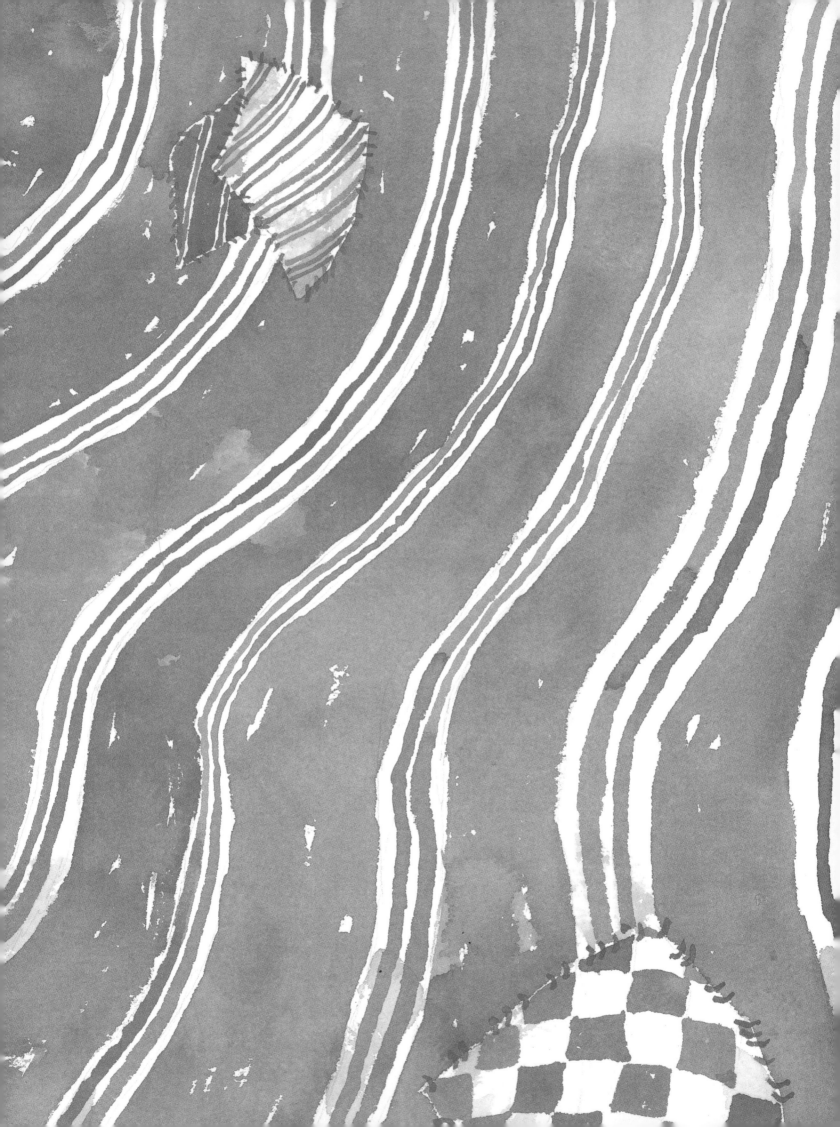

for James

The Sea House

may you always have a good handbook...

Deborah Turney Zagwÿn

TRICYCLE PRESS
BERKELEY / TORONTO

In memory of Uncle Wim, whose passion for art

TRICYCLE PRESS
A little division of Ten Speed Press
P.O. Box 7123
Berkeley, California 94707
www.tenspeed.com

Uncle Hal's knots are from *The Complete Book of Knots* by Geoffrey Budworth (The Lyons Press, 1997). Walt Whitman quotation is from *The Saturday Evening Post Book of the Sea and Ships* (The Curtis Publishing Company, 1978).

Book design by Tasha Hall
Typeset in Carlton, Caslon Antique, and Optima

Library of Congress Cataloging-in-Publication Data
Zagwyn, Deborah Turney.
  The sea house / Deborah Turney Zagwyn.
    p. cm.
  Summary: Uncle Fishtank Hal takes Clee and Simon aboard his barge, and after trouble with some pesky knots they find themselves at sea.
  ISBN 1-58246-030-2
  [1. Boats and boating—Fiction. 2. Barges—Fiction. 3. Uncles—Fiction.] I. Title.
PZ7.Z245 Se 2002   2001004574
[E]—dc21

First printing, 2002.
Printed in Singapore

1 2 3 4 5 6 7 — 06 05 04 03 02

and poetry was as big as the sea

To me the sea is a continual miracle,
The fishes that swim—the rocks—the motion
   of the waves—the ships with the men in them,
What stranger miracles are there?
                                      —WALT WHITMAN

N

W   E

S

The truck purred and then its sound faded altogether. Clee and Simon faced the sea with their uncle, Fishtank Hal.

Uncle Hal squinted at Clee. He winked at Simon. His face had more wrinkles and bristles than Clee remembered and his clothes looked ready for the laundry bucket.

"Follow me, Crew," Uncle Hal offered each a burly hand and they clump clump clumped to where his barge bumped against the dock.

"She's held fast with mooring knots and such," he said.

Clee stared at the barge. It tipped a bit to one side. This was not the boat Uncle Hal had talked about in his visits. It couldn't be.

"Come in, be welcome!" Uncle Hal boomed. Inside, his cabin smelled of fried fish and sweaty socks.

"You do have fishbowls for windows!" Clee exclaimed, peering in tank after tank. Only one held water, half full and murky. It housed two small shells.

"But, no fish," she said.

"They're hermit crabs," Uncle Hal told her. "I found them in me motor casing waiting for the propeller to give them another whirl."

At dinner Uncle Hal whirled around his tiny kitchen. He cooked a pot of snapper stew but dropped it when the rope handles gave way.

"Dratted loop knots," he fumed. "Back to me sailor handbook. Pocket-sized, it is. Says here…"

A loop knot makes a strong secure loop with any rope, big or small. Good for handles or attaching fishing tackle.

That night Uncle Hal unrolled three hammocks and tied them to the corners of the cabin.

"Scaffold knots, every one of them," he boasted.

The hermit crabs were tucking themselves in. Clee could see that their shells were too small for them. Their efforts stirred up the sand.

"Me Great-Uncle Harry Houdini, the escape artist, knew all about tight places," said Uncle Hal. "Hop in yer bags and I'll spin you a bedtime yarn."

"Harry, who could undo every lock and wriggle out of every knot known to man, was lashed in a straitjacket and lowered headfirst into a tank of water.

"Imagine," said Uncle Hal, "That your sleeping bag is wrapped around you and you can't get free."

Clee didn't like the idea at all.

"Imagine," continued Uncle Hal, climbing into his bed, "That you are Harry Houdini and you are straining in your straitjacket, holding yer breath."

Outside a chain was rattling on the deck.

"It's Harry!" whispered Simon.

"While the clock is ticking away yer remaining minutes and all of a sudden...."

KERTHUMP! Uncle Hal's hammock dropped to the cabin floor.

KERTHUMP! Simon's followed.

Simon gasped. Then he took a deep breath and let out a bellow.

"Drat!" groaned Uncle Hal. "Are you in one piece, Simon? Blasted scaffold knots. Back to me sailor handbook. Pocket-sized and by me bedside, it is. Says here…"

A scaffold knot creates an adjustable loop—Good for hanging a net bed from the ceiling.

"Come, Simon," Clee said, "I can squeeze over. There's room in my hammock for both of us."

She wondered if her bed would hold fast. Uncle Hal's knots were full of promises before they let you down.

Clee was not herself the next day or the day after. She was not the girl who followed her uncle everywhere or who laughed at his stories.

"Come out, Clee!" Simon was rolling a large spool down the deck.

"Later!" she called back to him. Why hadn't he noticed that Uncle Hal's barge was barely floating and that Uncle Hal's house was disorderly and that Uncle Hal was not much of a sailor at all?

Uncle Hal pointed out that Clee was missing the tides pulling out
the sea and pushing it in again.

"Over and over, every day, like magic," he told her.

Clee watched the hermit crabs pulling and pushing their shells
around and said nothing.

At the end of the first week Clee felt the barge lifting. Uncle Hal was pumping and patching its sunken side.

"So me pots don't roll around in significant weather," he announced. "Next, I'll tinker on that heap of a motor."

What for? Clee thought. This boat is going nowhere.

Then, sperlash! It was a Simon-sized splash.

Clee scrambled over the deck. Simon had been flip-flopping like a snapper, on the gangplank rope, when the ties gave way. Clee watched Fishtank Hal dangle from the railing to drag her sputtering brother out.

"Anchor bend knots, be durned!"

Clee glared at her uncle. Simon had lost a shoe and his toes stirred the puddle at his feet.

"Back to me pocket-sized handbook," Uncle Hal stammered.
"Says here…"

An anchor bend knot makes a secure hitch in wet and slimy conditions—Good for handrails.

Clee rolled up in her bedding long before bedtime. In the night she woke and saw the moon floating on a fog bank. Something was different. The hermit crabs were huddled in their shells. Uncle Hal and Simon were curled in their hammocks. But something was missing. Then Clee knew. The sound of the barge rubbing against the dock was gone.

"Uncle Hal!" Clee sat up. "We're sailing!"

Uncle Hal flew out of bed. He threw open the door and burst onto the deck. The slap of the sea greeted him. No dock in sight.

"Where's me sailor handbook?" he moaned. "Dratted pocket-sized answer to everything. It would say…"

A mooring knot is a medieval hitch knot. Simple to tie—Good for Incompetents and Simpletons!

Fishtank Hal whacked his forehead with the palm of his hand.

"Well, Crew, our engine is a bit finicky, but we've a piece of canvas for a sail. Clee, fetch me sailor handbook, while I wrestle with the ropes for a bit."

Breakfast that morning was served on a map.

"The wind will steer us that way with the help of the tide." Uncle Hal circled the closest bay with his fork.

Uncle Hal tied his canvas sail to the barge pole with a variety of foolproof knots and hitches. He double-tied them. He triple-tied them. He added extra ropes and even a chain for weight. He asked Clee to read aloud parts of his sailor handbook as he fiddled and looped and tucked and twisted and pulled.

Simon helped by blowing very hard. At first the wind was playing elsewhere but then the big canvas sail filled.

Like a cheek, thought Clee.

The sail arced and spurred the barge around the inlet.

The barge pole's ropes held fast. As they sailed, Fishtank Hal worked on his motor. Clee called out instructions from the manual while Simon lined up the wrenches and dropped a few overboard. The engine was almost ship-shape when the barge scraped to a halt.

"Well I'll be blessed!" Uncle Hal peered over the railing. "We've rubbed ourselves up against a sandbar. No need for me sailor handbook."

He tweaked Clee under the chin, "No need to worry either. Next tide will lift us on our way."

"Which way?" wondered Clee. But then she knew it really didn't matter. Uncle Hal's flat-bottomed boat was just resting, waiting for the tide to turn.

"Aye, aye, captain!" she said.

That afternoon, Clee and Simon explored the beach and beyond.
With the surf out, the ribbed sand and steaming rock pools offered
endless treasures—starfish and limpets, sponges and urchins,
mussels and seaweed, kelp and abalone.

"Brought you two a pair of troublemakers." Uncle Hal set a
bucket down next to Clee and grinned.

"They're jumping ship!"

Clee tipped the bucket into a pool at her feet. The hermit crabs settled next to a pair of very fine dogwinkle shells. After some tapping and measuring with their claws, they squeezed out of the old shells and slid into the new.

"Now it's up to the sea," said Uncle Hal. "Soon high tide will spill into every last pool. Fresh food. Clean water. Aye, it's as simple and complicated as that. Well, Crew, we'd best be getting back to me barge."

Clee could see the surf approaching now. It was streaming over the sandy bay to the barge, reaching for it. Soon it would cover the rocks and spill into the hermit crab pool. But by then Clee and Simon would be afloat.

Maybe Uncle Hal's boat was a dogwinkle barge, Clee thought. A strange house, different at first, but once you got used to it, it felt like home.

Clee looked up at her uncle. His sailor handbook was snug in his vest pocket. His eyes reflected the sea.

As they picked their way along a shrinking path back to the barge,
Clee's voice rose above the rolling of the water.

"The sea is swallowing the sun, Uncle Hal."

"That pesky sun always sets the sky afire at the end of the day,"
he said. "Lucky for us, the sea pulls 'er down and quenches 'er at
night, then spits 'er out to shine again in the morning."

"Over and over, every day," Clee said, "like magic."

About Hermit Crabs

Hermit crabs live in borrowed shells: discarded mollusks, like whelks and periwinkles.

When hermit crabs outgrow their shells, they find larger ones. They tap them (to make sure they are unoccupied) and measure them (to make sure they are a good size) and shake out any sand and pebbles inside (to ensure a clean house). Then they back their soft abdomens into these new abodes.

Hermit crabs often pair up with anemones (who attach themselves to the top of the crabs' shells). This is a great arrangement. Anemones protect the crabs from predators, and in return the hermit crabs help feed them. When the crabs move into bigger shells, they take their anemones with them. They are kind to their anemones!

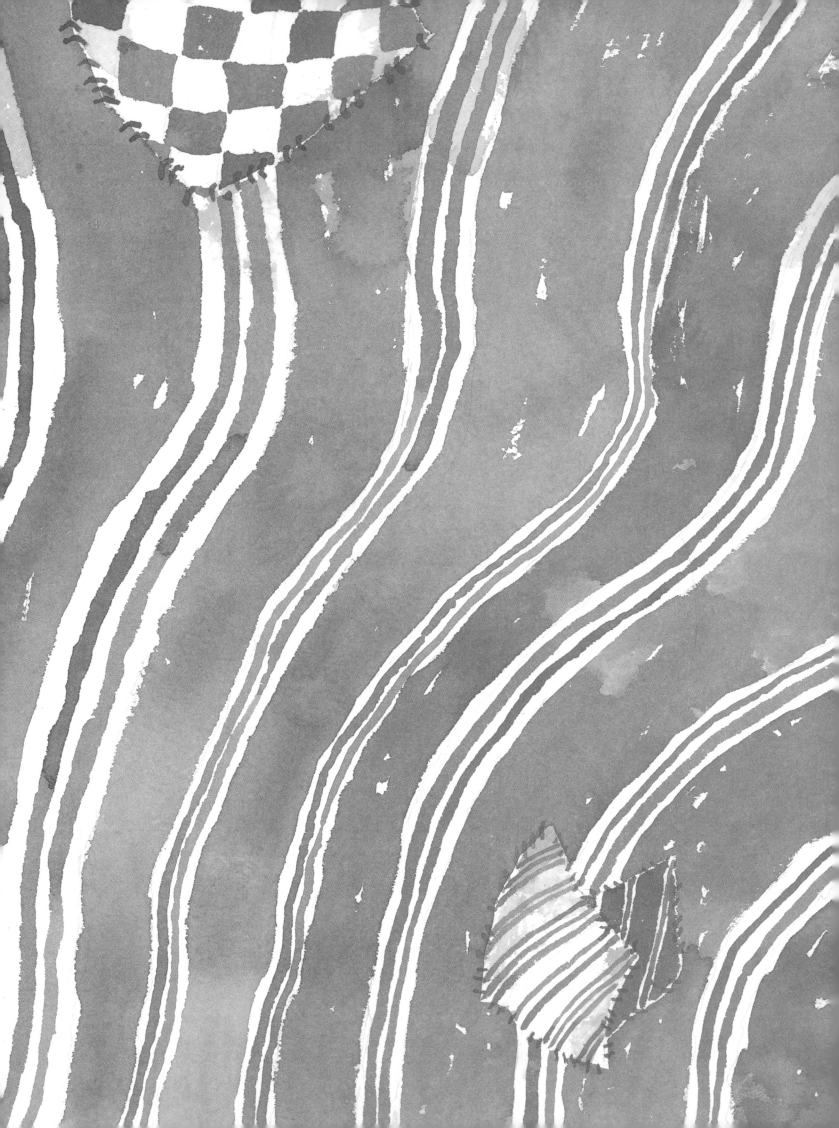